HarperCollins®, ☖®, and HarperFestival®
are trademarks of HarperCollins Publishers.
The Tall Book of Fairies
Illustrations copyright © 2007 Aleksey and Olga Ivanov
All new material copyright © 2007 by HarperCollins Publishers.
Manufactured in China. All rights reserved.
For information address HarperCollins Children's Books, a division of HarperCollins Publishers,
1350 Avenue of the Americas, New York, NY 10019.
Library of Congress catalog card number: 2006939821
www.harpercollinschildrens.com
Book design by Joe Merkel
❖
First HarperFestival edition, 2007

The Tall Book of Fairies

ILLUSTRATED BY ALEKSEY & OLGA IVANOV

ADAPTED BY
JENNY BAK AND LAURA MARCHESANI

HarperFestival®
A Division of HarperCollins*Publishers*

Anna

Table of Contents

TOADS AND DIAMONDS

Once upon a time, a widow lived with two
girls. The eldest girl was the widow's
true daughter, and the youngest was her
stepdaughter. The widow and her daughter
were as alike as two eggs in the same nest.
They were both lazy and cruel.

The youngest girl, who was kind and
intelligent, was also one of the most beautiful girls ever seen. But the widow treated
only her own daughter well, and they both
took delight in making the days and nights
miserable for the poor stepdaughter.

Among other things, she was forced twice
a day to draw water from a faraway spring.

Early one day, as she was fetching water from this fountain, an old woman in rags approached her and begged for a drink.

"Of course, ma'am," said the girl. She took up some water from the clearest place in the fountain and gave it to the old woman, holding up the pitcher so that she might drink more easily.

The old woman drank her fill and said to the girl, "My dear, you are so very good that I cannot help giving you a gift." For this was a fairy who had disguised herself to test how well people treated those less fortunate or able. "For your gift," continued the fairy, "at every word you speak, there shall come out of your mouth either a lovely flower or a precious jewel."

The young girl thanked the fairy sweetly and hurried home with her heavy pitcher of water. When she came home, the widow scolded her for staying so long at the fountain.

"I beg your pardon for not coming back sooner," said the poor girl humbly. And there rolled out of her mouth two roses, two pearls, and two diamonds!

"What is it I see there?" said the widow, quite astonished. "How did this happen?"

As the girl told her entire tale, dozens of diamonds and roses spilled onto the rough wooden floor. The widow's eyes gleamed with greed as she heard the story, and she called the eldest girl to come.

"I must send you to the spring right away!" the widow said. "Look what happens when your stepsister speaks. You should have the same gift, too, or better! All you have to do is fetch water from the spring, and when a certain poor woman asks you to let her drink, give it to her very nicely."

But the lazy daughter tossed her hair and replied, "I'd rather not. The spring is too far." But the widow insisted until the girl gave in. Away she went, grumbling all the way, taking with her the best silver pitcher in the house.

She was no sooner at the fountain than she saw coming out of the wood a lady most gloriously dressed, who came up to her and asked to drink. This was the very fairy who had appeared to the younger girl, but now had taken on the air and dress of a princess to see how she would be treated.

The lazy daughter laughed mockingly at the fairy's request. "Have I come all this way just to serve you water?" She sneered. "You'll have to stay thirsty, for I'm waiting for a fairy disguised as an old woman."

"You are not kind or good," answered the fairy calmly. "Since you have so few manners, for a gift I grant you that at every word you speak there shall come out of your mouth a snake or a toad." And with that, the fairy vanished in a puff of smoke.

Soon, the widow spied her daughter approaching the house. She hurried out to meet her and asked, "Well, Daughter?"

"Well, Mother?" the eldest girl rudely answered, as a viper and a toad jumped from her mouth.

"Oh!" cried the mother. "What is it I see? It's your wretched stepsister who has caused this trouble, and she shall pay for it!" Immediately, the widow ran to beat the innocent girl. The poor child fled away and hid herself in the forest, crying bitterly.

The king's son, returning from a hunting trip, passed by on his horse and saw the pretty young girl. He asked her what she was doing in the forest and why she cried.

"Alas!" the girl replied. "My stepmother has turned me out of the house." And as she spoke, five pearls and as many diamonds came out of her mouth. Enchanted, the prince begged her to continue her story. She told him the whole tale, and soon he fell in love with her goodness and beauty. He asked the young girl to be his wife, to which she happily agreed. Together they went back to his castle, where they married and lived happily ever after.

ALADDIN AND THE
MAGIC LAMP

Once upon a time, there lived a poor young man. One day, a grandly dressed stranger asked him if his name was Aladdin. "It is, sir," he replied.

The stranger exclaimed, "I am your uncle and have returned from traveling through faraway lands. You are my nephew and my only heir. Come with me." The stranger, who was not really Aladdin's uncle but an evil magician, led Aladdin far outside the city gates until they came to two mountains divided by a narrow valley. The magician lit a fire and threw powder on the flames while saying magical words. The earth trembled a little and opened in front of them, revealing steps leading into darkness.

The magician turned to the frightened Aladdin and said, "In there lies a treasure that is to be yours, but you must do exactly as I tell you. At the foot of the steps you will find a door. Walk on until you come to a lighted lamp. Bring it to me."

Aladdin forgot his fear and descended into the cavern. He quickly fetched the lamp. The magician, waiting outside, insisted that the lamp be handed up to him, but Aladdin would not give up the lamp until he was out of the cave. The evil magician became angry at this and threw more powder onto the fire while reciting magical words. Suddenly, the ground closed up and trapped Aladdin inside the cavern!

Aladdin didn't know how to escape. While he tried to think of a plan, he absently rubbed the lamp that had cost him his freedom. Suddenly, from the lamp rose a genie, a magical spirit that can grant wishes. It said, "What is your wish?" Aladdin fearlessly replied, "Deliver me from this place!" With a tremble, the earth opened, and Aladdin found himself at home. He rubbed the lamp again and wished for food and money until he was quite rich.

One day, Aladdin saw the sultan's
daughter pass by and instantly fell in love
with her. He presented the sultan with
rich jewels and asked for the princess's
hand in marriage, but the sultan needed to
know if this stranger was worthy. "You
may marry my daughter if you can bring
me forty basins of gold and jewels by
tomorrow!" he declared. The next day,
Aladdin brought not forty but eighty
basins of gold and jewels and laid them
at the sultan's feet. Dazzled by the riches,
the sultan agreed to the marriage. The
wedding lasted for many days and nights,
with much feasting and rejoicing.

Aladdin built a beautiful palace decorated with gold and precious jewels. He and the princess lived there happily, not knowing that the evil magician had heard of the princess's fortunate marriage to a stranger named Aladdin, whose wealth was beyond compare. The magician knew that only the genie could be responsible for such lavish riches and vowed to get the lamp.

One day, Aladdin went away on a trip while his wife stayed at the palace. The magician bought a dozen copper lamps, put them into a basket, and went to the palace, crying, "New lamps for old!" Hearing this, the princess thought of the old, worn lamp that sat on a shelf in the bedroom. She brought it to the magician and said, "Give me a new lamp for this old one." He snatched it and went to a quiet place where he pulled out the lamp and rubbed it. The genie appeared and, at the magician's command, swept him and the palace with the princess inside to a faraway place.

When Aladdin returned, he found his palace and wife gone. For many days he wandered about like a madman, asking everyone what had become of his palace. Finally he found the palace and was secretly reunited with the unhappy princess. The magician kept asking her to marry him and was getting angry with every refusal she gave. Aladdin asked her about the lamp and learned that the magician carried it safely hidden in his clothing. Aladdin thought of a plan.

The next day, the princess put on her loveliest dress and went to see the magician. "I have given it much thought," she said. "I know now that I will never see Aladdin again, so I will marry you. But first, I want to share a glass of wine with you to celebrate." The magician ran to fetch a bottle of wine, and the princess put a sleeping powder into his cup. She insisted that he have the first sip, and the magician quickly

fell into a deep slumber. Instantly, Aladdin sprang through a window and retrieved the lamp from the magician. After he rubbed the lamp, the palace and its occupants were back in their rightful land in the blink of an eye, and the magician was placed in jail.

The sultan joyfully welcomed his daughter home and commanded there to be feasting for ten days to mark her safe return. The lamp was locked securely away, and Aladdin and his wife lived for many years in happiness and prosperity.

THE FROG PRINCE

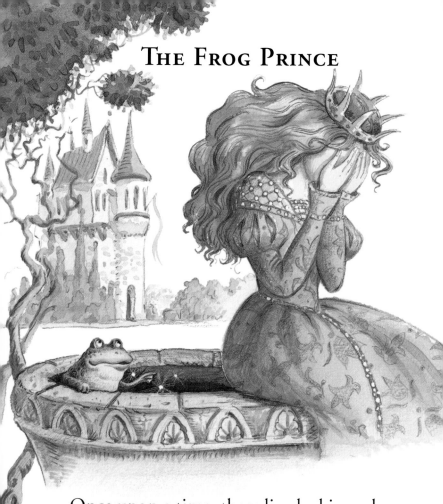

Once upon a time, there lived a king whose daughters were all beautiful, but the youngest was the most beautiful of all. On warm days, the youngest princess liked to sit by the side of a nearby well. When she was bored she would throw a golden ball, her favorite toy, up high and catch it.

One day, the princess's ball rolled straight into the water. She looked inside, but the well was so deep that the bottom could not be seen. She began to cry until a voice said, "What ails you, Princess? You weep so that even a stone would show pity."

The princess looked around and saw a frog stretching forth his big, ugly head from the water.

"I am weeping for my golden ball, which has fallen into the well," she said.

"Do not weep," answered the frog. "I can help you, but what will you give me if I bring your ball up again?"

"Whatever you want, dear frog," said she, "my clothes, my pearls and jewels, and even the golden crown that I am wearing."

The frog answered, "I do not want anything but for you to love me and let me be your friend, and let me sit by you at your little table, and eat off your little golden plate, and drink out of your little cup, and sleep in your little bed. If you will promise me this, I will bring your golden ball up again."

"Oh, yes," said she, "I promise you all you wish, if you will but bring me my ball back again." But she thought, *As if a silly frog could really be a person's friend!*

The frog dove into the water and retrieved the ball. The delighted princess picked it up and ran quickly away.

"Wait!" called the frog. "Take me with you. I can't run as fast as you!" But the princess ran to the castle without looking back.

The next day, while she was dining with the king and all the courtiers, something crept *splish-splash, splish-splash* up the marble staircase, and then knocked at the door and cried, "Princess, open the door for me!" She ran to open the door, and there sat the ugly frog. Frightened, she slammed the door and sat down to dinner again. The king saw plainly that she was afraid and said to her, "Daughter, why are you so afraid? Is there perchance a giant outside who wants to carry you away?"

"It is no giant but a disgusting frog," replied the princess. She explained what had happened at the well. In the meantime, the frog knocked a second time and called for her again.

The king said, "What you promised, you must do. Go and let him in." She went and opened the door, and the frog hopped in and followed her, step by step, to her chair. And so the frog sat by her at the table, ate off her little golden plate, and drank out of her little cup. The frog enjoyed himself, but almost every spoonful the princess ate choked her. After dinner, he said, "Now I am tired. Carry me into your little room, and we will both lie down and go to sleep."

The king's daughter began to cry, for she was afraid of the cold frog and did not want him to sleep in her pretty, clean little bed. But the king grew angry and said, "He helped you when you were in trouble and should not be despised by you now." So she took hold of the frog with two fingers, carried him into her room, and put him on her bed.

The frog said, "Now give me a goodnight kiss or I will tell your father." The princess shut her eyes and kissed the frog on his clammy cheek. When she opened her eyes, he was no longer a frog but a king's son, with kind and beautiful eyes. The prince told her how he had been bewitched by an evil fairy to live as a frog, and how no one could have delivered him from the well but herself. The next day, the prince and princess celebrated a joyful wedding and went together to rule his kingdom and live happily ever after.

PETER PAN

Late one night, Peter Pan and the fairy
Tinker Bell flew across the London sky.
They stopped at the window outside the
nursery of the Darling house and crept
inside. Peter was looking for his shadow.
He had left it behind the last time he
visited the nursery, when he secretly
listened to Wendy Darling tell bedtime
stories about his home, Neverland, to her
brothers, Michael and John.

Finally, Peter found his shadow. After he caught it, he tried to sew it back on, but that didn't work. Peter started to cry, which woke up Wendy. She could not believe her eyes. A boy and a fairy were flying around her room!

"Don't be frightened," Peter said. "Will you come to Neverland with me and tell your stories to my friends? I'll teach you to fly!"

Wendy agreed only after he included John and Michael in the fantastic adventure. The fairy Tinker Bell sprinkled her fairy dust over the children, and soon they were all soaring through the sky and over the sea.

"Second to the right, and straight on till morning!" Peter shouted. When they reached Neverland, they found a beautiful island with golden rainbows, blue waterfalls, the Mermaids' Lagoon, and a pirate ship where the evil Captain Hook lived.

Peter Pan took the children to meet his friends, the lost boys. At the Mermaids' Lagoon, Peter saw that Captain Hook had captured the beautiful Princess Tiger Lily. Peter followed Captain Hook to Marooners' Rock, where they had a duel. Peter made

Captain Hook fall into the sea, where he was chased away by a crocodile. Tiger Lily was saved!

That wasn't the end of Captain Hook. He kidnapped Tinker Bell and tricked her into telling him the location of Peter's home. He led his band of pirates to capture the lost boys and the Darling children.

Tinker Bell was imprisoned in the pirate ship, but escaped just in time to alert Peter. She knew that Hook had put poison in Peter's cup, but Peter would not believe her. As he was about to drink it, Tinker Bell quickly flew and drank it all herself. Suddenly, she dropped to the ground, with her light fading rapidly.

"Oh, Tink, did you drink it to save me?" Peter cried. "How can I help you?"

Tinker Bell said weakly, "I can get well again if children believed in fairies."

Peter wasted no time. He thought of the many children who were dreaming of Neverland at that moment, and asked of them all, "Do you believe?" Tinker Bell heard the children murmur "Yes!" in their sleep and felt much better. She was saved!

Peter and the fairy flew to Captain Hook's pirate ship, where the Darlings and the lost boys were walking the plank. Wendy had just stepped off and was falling into the ocean! Peter swooped in just in time and rescued her, and then began a fierce duel with Captain Hook. Once again, the evil Hook fell into the water and was chased away by the crocodile—this time forever.

Tinker Bell sprinkled her fairy dust on the ship, and suddenly it was flying through the skies of Neverland, on its way to London. Back in the nursery, Peter Pan and Tinker Bell said good-bye to the children and sailed off into the night. Wendy watched as the beautiful ship sailed past the moon on its journey home to Neverland, the most wonderful land of her dreams.

THE GOOD LITTLE MOUSE

Once upon a time, an evil king invaded another kingdom and captured the queen and her infant daughter. He shut them both into the highest room of the tallest tower in the castle. The room was small and empty, with only one table and a very hard bed on the floor. The wicked king sent for a fairy, who was so moved by the prisoners' misery that she whispered to the queen, "Courage, Madam! I think I see a way to help you."

"Silence!" the king cried. He turned to the fairy. "Tell me, is this baby girl destined to grow up to be a worthy bride for my son?"

The fairy answered that the princess would be kind and beautiful. Satisfied, the king declared that the queen would raise the baby in the tower until the girl was old enough to marry his son. Then he took the fairy with him and left the poor queen in tears.

As the days went on, the queen and her baby grew thinner and thinner, for every day they were given only three peas and a crust of black bread to eat. One evening, as the queen sat at her spinning wheel—for she was made to work day and night—she saw a pretty little mouse creep out of a hole. She said to the mouse, "Alas, little creature! Why did you come here? I have only three peas to eat each day, so unless you wish to starve, I'm afraid you must go elsewhere for your food."

But the mouse danced and twirled so prettily that the queen clapped and laughed and gave the mouse her last pea, which she was keeping for her supper.

Suddenly, a delicious meal appeared on the table. The queen was amazed! Quickly she fed her baby and herself and gave the mouse its own share.

The next day, and every day after that, the queen gave the mouse all of the peas, and instantly the empty dish was filled with all sorts of wonderful things to eat. But the queen still worried about the fate of her daughter. The queen despaired and said, "If only I could think of some way of saving her from marrying the horrible prince!"

As she spoke, she noticed the little mouse playing in a corner with some long straws. The queen began to braid the straws, thinking, *If I had enough straws, I could make a basket to lower my baby down from the window. A kind passerby might take care of her and raise her in freedom.*

As she sat braiding, the little mouse dragged in more and more straw, until the queen had plenty to weave her basket. At last, the basket was finished. The queen went to the window to see how long a cord she must make and noticed an old woman far below, looking up at her. The

old woman called to the queen, "I know your trouble, Madam. If you like, I will help you."

The queen was overjoyed and told the old woman that she would be rewarded for her kindness.

"I don't care about any reward," the old woman replied. "'But there is one thing I should like. I am very particular about what I eat, and I fancy above all else a plump, tender little mouse. If there happens to be any mouse in your garret, just throw it down to me. That's all I ask."

The queen began to cry. "There is only one mouse in this garret," said the queen, "but I cannot bear to think of its being killed."

"What!" cried the old woman, in a rage. "You care more for a miserable mouse than for your very own baby? Good-bye, Madam! I leave you and your poor daughter to enjoy its company!"

That night, the queen sadly placed the baby in the basket and prepared to lower it into the street. Just then, in sprang the little mouse.

"Oh, little mouse!" said the queen. "It cost me dear to save your life."

Suddenly, the mouse answered, "Believe me, Madam, you will never regret your kindness."

The queen was astonished when the mouse began to speak, and still more so when the mouse suddenly grew into a tall, fair lady. The queen recognized the fairy who had come up to her tower room with the wicked king.

The fairy smiled at her astonished look and said, "I wanted to see if you were faithful and capable of real friendship before

I helped you. You see, we fairies are rich in everything but friends, and those are hard to find. I was the little mouse whom you fed when there was nothing to be gained by it. I was the old woman whom you talked to from the window. You are indeed capable of true friendship." Turning to the princess, she said, "Dear little one, I promise you and your mother will be safe under my care. Let us live happily together in my castle, far from here."

The fairy then cast a spell, and all three vanished from the prison room, never to see the wicked king again.

Fairer-than-a-Fairy

Once there lived a king and queen who had no children. Finally, a daughter was born to them, and she was such a beautiful baby that the king named her Fairer-than-a-Fairy.

When the fairies heard this name, they became jealous of the little princess. They gathered together and decided to take the baby away from the king as punishment for his pride. The fairies chose Lagree to fulfill the task. She was the oldest of the fairies and had only one eye and one tooth. As evil as she was old, Lagree snatched Fairer-than-a-Fairy from the king's castle and brought her to live in a splendid palace with a pet cat and dog to keep her company. When the princess was seven years old, Lagree ordered her to keep alive the fire that was burning brightly in her room. Ten years passed, during which time Fairer-than-a-Fairy grew accustomed to her lonely life and obeyed Lagree's orders, all the while never knowing that she was a princess.

One day, while passing near a fountain in the garden, she noticed that the sun's rays fell on the water to create a brilliant rainbow. As she looked at it, she heard a young man's voice speaking to her from within its shining colors. The rainbow informed Fairer-than-a-Fairy that he was a young prince and that the fairy Lagree had enchanted him after his parents had angered her. The prince could speak only as a rainbow, and so it was necessary that the sun should shine on water to let the rainbow form.

Fairer-than-a-Fairy soon spent all her days by the fountain, conversing with the prince about everything. One day, the princess forgot to attend to the fire, and it went out. Lagree, upon discovering this, punished Fairer-than-a-Fairy severely.

After this, the princess decided it was too dangerous to leave the fire alone. So every morning, she placed a large basin full of water on her windowsill, and as soon as the sun's rays fell on the water, the rainbow appeared as clearly as it had ever done in the fountain.

One day, Prince Rainbow unhappily told Fairer-than-a-Fairy that he was about to be banished to an unknown place. The princess vowed to travel every land until she found him, and she set off immediately, taking nothing with her but her dog and cat.

When Lagree realized the princess had fled, she set off at full speed in pursuit. As she reached the princess and was about to cast a spell, the little dog flew at Lagree and bit her on the leg. Fairer-than-a-Fairy escaped and continued her flight. But Lagree ran after her on one leg and soon caught up with the princess again.

This time, the cat sprang at Lagree and scratched her other leg so that she was unable to follow the princess anymore.

As she went on, Fairer-than-a-Fairy became overwhelmed with hunger and thirst. She dragged herself to a little green-and-white house, where she was received by a beautiful lady dressed in green and white. The kind lady fed the princess and let her rest, and in the morning she presented her with a perfume bottle to use when in need. After another day and night of walking, Fairer-than-a-Fairy was again exhausted and found another house exactly like the one she had just left. Here again she received a present, this time a golden pomegranate.

After a long time, the road led to a wonderful silver castle suspended by strong gold chains attached to two of the largest trees. It was so perfectly hung that a gentle breeze rocked it sufficiently to send its inhabitants pleasantly to sleep.

Fairer-than-a-Fairy felt that her rainbow prince must be held in this castle. She climbed a chain and reached a door, but no amount of knocking or calling would open it. In despair, she opened the perfume bottle to see what would happen. Out came a tiny golden key that opened the door effortlessly.

The princess entered a magnificent room lighted by gold and jeweled stars in the ceiling. In the midst of this room was a bed draped with curtains in all the colors of the rainbow. It was suspended by golden cords so that it swayed with the castle in a manner that rocked its occupant to sleep.

On this elegant bed lay the handsome Prince Rainbow, but no amount of shaking or shouting would awaken him from his deep slumber. After coming such a long way, Fairer-than-a-Fairy would not give up. She opened the pomegranate, and out of every seed flew a violin, until dozens floated in the air and played as loudly as they could. Prince Rainbow jumped awake and was overjoyed to find Fairer-than-a-Fairy at his side.

The green-and-white ladies, who were really fairies, arrived with the parents of Prince Rainbow and Fairer-than-a-Fairy to celebrate the end of Lagree's evil enchantments. A grand wedding took place that very night, and everyone lived happily ever after.

THE TWELVE BROTHERS

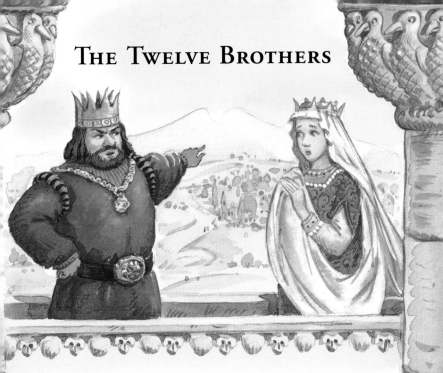

Once upon a time, a king and queen had twelve sons. One day, the king said to his wife, "If our thirteenth child is a girl, all her twelve brothers must be banished from the land, so that she may be very rich and the kingdom hers alone."

When the next baby was born, it was a little girl. The queen was sad to hear that she would no longer be able to see her dear sons and cried all day. Finally, her youngest son asked why she cried. The queen did not want to tell him, but he insisted until she finally spoke of the king's order.

"Don't cry, Mother," he said. "My brothers and I will hide nearby, and you can visit us when it's safe."

"Yes," replied his mother. "There is a cottage deep in the woods. Stay there with your brothers, and I will come when I can." Then she blessed her sons, and they set out into the wood. After walking a long time, they came upon a little enchanted house that stood empty.

"Let's live here," the brothers decided. To the youngest, they said, "You will stay home and keep house while we get food."

For ten years, the brothers lived in the cottage happily. Their mother slipped out to see them occasionally, but she could not convince the king to let them return from what he thought was their faraway exile. In the meantime, their little sister was growing up quickly. She was kind and fair, and she had a gold star right in the middle of her forehead, for which she was named. One day, Princess Star looked down from her window and saw her mother washing twelve men's shirts. She asked her mother whom they belonged to.

The queen confessed the sad story, and the princess was determined to find her brothers. She entered the woods and walked all day long, until she reached the little house. She stepped in and found a youth who was surprised by her beauty and the golden star on her forehead, and he asked her where she was going.

"I am a princess," she answered, "and am seeking my twelve brothers. I mean to wander as far as the blue sky stretches over the earth till I find them."

Then the brother knew who she was, and they greeted each other happily. When the rest of the brothers came home that night, he cried, "Our sister is here!" and the princess stepped forward. With her sweet nature and charming ways, the brothers soon forgot any bitterness and embraced their sister. She stayed at home with the youngest brother and helped him with the housework, while the rest of the brothers went out into the wood to fetch their food.

There was a little garden by the enchanted house, in which grew twelve tall lilies. One day, Princess Star plucked the twelve flowers, meaning to present one to each of her brothers. But hardly had she plucked the flowers when her brothers turned into twelve ravens who quickly flew away, and the house and garden vanished also.

The princess sat and cried until an old woman approached. "My child, what have you done?" she asked. "Why didn't you leave the flowers alone? An evil fairy enchanted them to represent your twelve brothers, who are now ravens."

The girl asked, sobbing, "How can I set them free?"

"There is only one way in the whole world," replied the old woman, who was really a good fairy in disguise. "But it is so difficult that it will never work. For seven years, you cannot speak a single word or laugh. If you do, they will die."

Then Princess Star said to herself, *If that is all, I am quite sure I can free my brothers.* So she climbed a high tree to avoid seeing people, and she never laughed or spoke.

One day, a king was hunting in the wood, and his dog began barking at the princess in the tree. When the king looked up and saw the beautiful girl with the golden star on her forehead, he was so enchanted by her beauty that he asked her to be his wife. She nodded in response. Then he climbed up the tree, lifted her down, put her on his horse, and brought her to his palace.

The marriage was celebrated with much pomp and ceremony, but the bride neither spoke nor laughed.

When they had lived a few years happily together, the king's mother, who was a wicked old woman, began to say evil things about the young queen. She accused her of committing many crimes, but the girl could say nothing to defend herself. Finally, the king was convinced of her guilt, and he reluctantly sentenced her to death.

As the young queen was being led to her death, the very last moment of the seven years arrived. A sudden rushing sound was heard, and twelve ravens appeared overhead. They swooped downward, and as soon as they touched the ground they turned into twelve young men.

The brothers released their sister from her chains and hugged her again and again. And now that she was able to speak, she told her story to the king and his court.

The king rejoiced greatly when he heard she was innocent and punished his mother for her lies. The young queen traveled to her father's kingdom and persuaded him to allow his sons to return. Afterward, both kingdoms lived happily ever.

PRINCESS CAT

In ancient China, there lived an emperor with three sons. The emperor was old and did not want to give up his throne, although his sons were old enough to rule. He decided to keep them too busy to think of succeeding him.

The king called his three sons together and told them that he would give up his crown to the son who found him the smallest dog. He gave each of his sons plenty of gold and told them to return in one year. The eldest prince was disappointed, since the crown would traditionally be passed down to him without competition from his brothers, but he was too polite to argue with his father. The next day, the three princes set out in different directions.

The youngest son was handsome, smart, and very brave. One evening, as he was riding through a forest, a storm suddenly broke. The prince saw a bright light ahead and followed it until he came upon a magnificent palace with walls of crystal and an enormous door encrusted with jewels. When he knocked, the door swung open, and the prince was pulled inside by dozens of invisible hands.

Though uneasy, the prince looked about and found rich clothes set out for him. Then the hands led him to a dinner table set for two. A beautiful snow white cat entered and introduced herself as Princess Cat. She offered the prince a lavish feast and plenty to drink.

The prince was impressed by Princess Cat's generosity and her marvelous castle. He spent the night, and the next day the prince and Princess Cat played games, hunted in the woods, and picnicked by a

waterfall. The prince had so much fun that he stayed the next night, and the next, and the next—until the entire year was almost up.

Luckily, Princess Cat remembered the emperor's contest. She gave the prince a tiny acorn and told him to take it to his father. The prince sadly rode away from Princess Cat's land, already missing her wonderful company.

At the emperor's palace, the two older brothers showed their small dogs. Then it was the young prince's turn. The prince opened the acorn and out jumped a perfect, tiny dog that was no bigger than a snowflake. The dog barked and danced in the palm of the emperor's hand.

The emperor was amazed at his son's gift, but still did not want to give up his throne. He offered his sons the last challenge. After one year, whoever brought back the most beautiful princess in all the land would be emperor.

The prince immediately returned to

Princess Cat. She welcomed him back with a feast and a dance. The pair spent many months fishing, reading aloud, and playing in the woods. As quickly as before, the prince's year was almost up, and he had not yet found a beautiful princess. Resting in front of a fireplace, he asked Princess Cat for advice.

"This is what you must do," Princess Cat said. "Cut my tail off and throw it into the fire."

The prince refused to do as Princess Cat requested. He loved her and did not want to harm her. Princess Cat promised the prince that she would not be hurt and that it would please her. Finally, the prince agreed and shut his eyes as he cut off Princess Cat's tail and threw it into the fire.

Lo and behold! Out of the fireplace stepped a beautiful princess with silken hair and sparkling robes. At that instant, an elegant winged lady flew into the room and embraced the princess. Seeing the prince's confusion, the princess explained that she had been turned into a cat after she refused to wed an ugly magician. The winged lady was Princess Cat's friend, a kind fairy who had ensured that the spell would one day be broken by a prince who loved her dearly.

The prince did love Princess Cat with all his heart, and the pair made plans to marry. The fairy brought the prince and Princess Cat in her flying palanquin back to his father's palace. The emperor was amazed at Princess Cat's incredible beauty and declared his youngest son the winner of the challenge.

But then Princess Cat interrupted the emperor. "I am the ruler of six kingdoms," she said, "and I would love nothing more than to share those kingdoms with you and your sons." Two kingdoms were given to each prince, and the emperor was overjoyed that he could continue to rule his own. The three brothers wed their princesses, and everyone in the land celebrated their happy marriages for many years to come.

PINOCCHIO

Once upon a time, there was a piece of wood. The old woodcarver, Geppetto, decided to make it into a puppet named Pinocchio. As he carved the eyes, they seemed to look back at him. When he made the mouth, it opened and laughed at him. And when Geppetto carved two legs, the wooden puppet jumped up and ran away!

On his journey, Pinocchio came to a house that was empty but for a Talking Cricket. The cricket warned the puppet, "Woe to those boys who rebel against their parents and run away from home. They will never come to any good in the world." Because of his hunger more than his conscience, Pinocchio returned to Geppetto and promised to behave and go to school. The kindly old man made school clothes for Pinocchio and even sold his only coat to buy the puppet a schoolbook.

The next morning, Pinocchio was on his way to school when he heard the laughter of a crowd and the beating of drums. He turned from the path to school and followed the noise to a puppet theater.

Pinocchio wanted to see the show, but admission was ten cents! And although he promised Geppetto that he would be a good boy, Pinocchio traded his schoolbook for ten cents and went inside! The showman of the theater heard Pinocchio's story about Geppetto's sacrifice and said, "Here are five gold pieces. Go at once and take them to him with my compliments." Pinocchio was overjoyed and thanked the showman a thousand times. On his way back home, the puppet made the mistake of mentioning his newfound riches to Fox and Cat, an unscrupulous pair he met along the path. They chased Pinocchio through the woods, intent on robbing him, until he came to a house where a lovely Fairy with blue hair lived. There he rested in safety, and presently the Fairy came to visit with him. Pinocchio told her his story.

"Where are the gold pieces now?" she asked.

"I lost them!" the puppet lied. Suddenly, his nose grew two inches longer!

The Fairy asked, "Where did you lose them?"

"In the woods," he answered. At this second lie, his nose grew even more.

"Then we shall find them," the Fairy said. Pinocchio became afraid and stammered, "I mean that I swallowed them!" And his nose grew so long that the Fairy laughed at the sight. Pinocchio was so ashamed that he began to cry. After a while, the Fairy clapped her hands and one thousand woodpeckers came through the window and landed on his nose. They pecked at it until his nose was reduced to a normal size. Pinocchio was overjoyed! He thanked the Fairy and once more started on the path back to Geppetto's house. Again, he was interrupted on his journey, but this time a kind pigeon told him that

Geppetto had gone to the seashore to sail to distant lands and find Pinocchio.

Hearing this, Pinocchio felt saddened and guilty. He resolved again to behave and set out for the seashore. However, his lazy and idle nature got him into trouble yet again. He met a boy named Candlewick, who told him of a wonderful land just for boys. "There are no schools, no books, and the week consists of six Saturdays and one Sunday. The boys play from morning to night. That is the country for me!

Why don't you come, too?"

Pinocchio said no again and again, but when the coach arrived to take Candlewick to the wonderful land, he could not resist jumping on. Once there, he forgot about Geppetto and the Fairy and spent months playing and making mischief. One day, he woke up and looked in the mirror to find that he had grown donkey ears! He had caught donkey fever because he had been so idle, and soon he would become a whole donkey. The coachman who brought the boys to the land waited for each one to become a donkey, and then he sold them off to be used for work. He lured new boys with the promise of idleness and fun and now was rich from his evil scheme.

Within hours, Pinocchio was a full donkey and could only bray his sadness. He was quickly sold to a man who brought him to his home close to the seashore. Once there, Pinocchio ran away into the ocean and found that the water transformed him back into a puppet! Delighted, he swam away from his angry owner, farther into the sea.

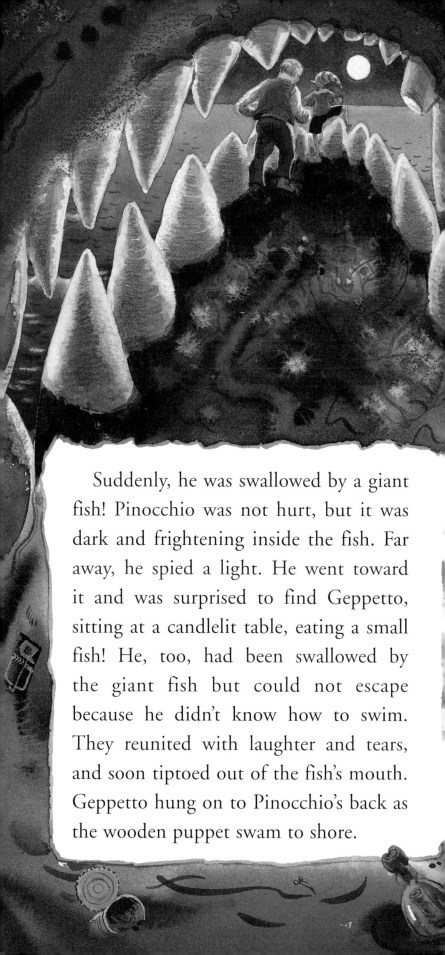

Suddenly, he was swallowed by a giant fish! Pinocchio was not hurt, but it was dark and frightening inside the fish. Far away, he spied a light. He went toward it and was surprised to find Geppetto, sitting at a candlelit table, eating a small fish! He, too, had been swallowed by the giant fish but could not escape because he didn't know how to swim. They reunited with laughter and tears, and soon tiptoed out of the fish's mouth. Geppetto hung on to Pinocchio's back as the wooden puppet swam to shore.

Once back at home, Pinocchio behaved as well as any real boy could. He went to school, took a job to earn money, and obeyed Geppetto without protest. One night, the Fairy appeared to him in a dream and praised his good deeds. "Well done, Pinocchio!" she said. "You will be rewarded for your good heart." When he awoke the next morning, Pinocchio found that he was a real boy! The rickety old house had also been changed to a warm and comfortable home, and even Geppetto seemed younger and livelier. "This is because of your good behavior," declared Geppetto. They danced with joy, and together they lived happily ever after.

THUMBELINA

There was once a woman whose greatest desire was to have a child. She went to see a fairy about her wish and received a flower seed, which she planted that night. The next morning, a beautiful red-and-gold flower with tightly closed petals had grown in the pot. The delighted woman kissed the bud, and suddenly the petals opened. Inside sat a very delicate and graceful little girl. She was the size of a thumb, and so she was named Thumbelina. Her cradle was a walnut shell, her bed was lined with violet leaves, and she had a rose petal for a blanket.

One night, an ugly toad crept through the window and leaped upon the table where Thumbelina lay sleeping. "What a pretty little wife she would make for my son," said the toad, and she took Thumbelina's bed and jumped through the window with it into the garden.

The toad took the cradle to the pond and placed it on a lily pad, and then went to fetch her son. Thumbelina awoke and cried at finding herself in a strange place with nowhere to go. The fish felt pity for the beautiful girl and nibbled on the lily stem so that she could escape from the toad's ugly son. Away down a stream floated the leaf on which Thumbelina sat, until a may bug picked her up and set her down in a meadow to live among the flowers and grasses.

All through the summer, Thumbelina ate blossom nectar and drank the rainwater that collected on leaves. She wove herself a bed from grasses and sang along with the birds that lived in the trees above. But autumn came, and then winter, and poor Thumbelina grew cold and hungry after the grasses died and the bitter wind began to blow. And when the snow came, each snowflake that landed on her was like a shovelful of snow thrown upon someone our size. Miserably, she left her meadow and wandered in search of food, until she came upon a field mouse's den. Thumbelina begged for a bit of food, and the good mouse took pity on the girl and welcomed Thumbelina into her home, where they lived very comfortably.

One day during the winter, the field mouse told Thumbelina that they would soon have a visitor and that she should prepare her prettiest stories to tell. "He is very rich, with a house twenty times larger than mine," said the mouse. "He is blind, but does very well." And so Thumbelina dutifully recited her best stories and sang her prettiest songs to the visitor, who was a mole. She did not like him, however, because he spoke badly of the sun, the flowers, and all the dear creatures she had lived with in the meadow. Being a mole, he preferred to live underground and rarely saw the daylight.

At the end of his visit, the mole guided Thumbelina and the field mouse through one of the tunnels that led to his house. He warned them that a dead bird lay along the passage. It was a large swallow with its wings drawn in tight and its eyes closed. After the mole and mouse had moved on, Thumbelina ran back to lay a warm blanket on the bird, so that even in death it would not be cold. As she straightened the blanket, she heard a weak *thump thump* in the swallow's chest. It was alive! Thumbelina was frightened but returned that night to cover the swallow with another blanket. Presently, the swallow awoke. "Thank you, pretty maiden," it croaked feebly. "I have been nicely warmed and shall soon regain my strength." All through the winter, Thumbelina secretly fed and nursed the bird back to health. In the springtime, the swallow prepared to leave the tunnel and asked her to join him, but Thumbelina could not leave the kind field mouse. When the swallow said good-bye and soared into the warm sunlight, Thumbelina felt very sad.

Returning to the field mouse's den, Thumbelina was surprised to see her so excited. "We must start working on your wedding clothes, dear!" said the mouse. "The mole has asked to marry you. You're a very lucky girl." Thumbelina had no choice but to sew a wedding dress. She did not want to marry the mole and live in his underground tunnels. She would miss the sun and the sky, as well as the birds and butterflies who cheered her days last summer.

At last, it was her wedding day. Thumbelina asked permission to stand at the door and say farewell to the daylight. As she stood in the sunshine with her arms raised, she heard a familiar *tweet tweet* overhead. It was her dear swallow! And when he asked her now if she would come with him, she agreed. On and on he flew,

until at last he landed near a beautiful lake where a dazzling white palace stood. His nest was among the top of the pillars, but he set Thumbelina down upon a flower of her choosing, where she would be safe.

To her surprise, a tiny man already stood on the flower, with a gold crown on his head and gossamer wings on his back. He was the prince of all flowers and ruled over all the tiny men and women who lived on each flower. The handsome fairy prince was delighted with Thumbelina, as she was the prettiest and sweetest girl he had ever met. He quickly put his crown on her head and asked her to be his wife. This bridegroom was different from the toad and the mole! Thumbelina agreed, and they celebrated their wedding that day. The swallow sang his loveliest song, and the other flower fairies came bearing wonderful gifts for their new princess. The best gift was a pair of fairy wings of her own, so that she could flit from flower to flower as well. Happiness had come to Thumbelina at last, and she and the prince rejoiced at their good fortune until the end of their days.